Usborne
Spotter's Guides
Wild Flowers

Sarah Russell

Illustrated by Mary Woodin

Designed by Sharon Cooper
Consultants: Sarah and Derek Niemann
Additional research by Kate Nolan

How to use this book

This guide is organized by colour, so it's easy to identify and learn about the flowers you find. There's also a calendar at the back of the book, where you can discover which ones to look out for in each season. Make sure you go spotting with a grown-up, and remember never to uproot any flowers, or touch any plants if you're not sure what they are. To help you identify the flowers, the pictures point out details like this...

Learning more

A fact box next to each wild flower tells you its botanical name (which is how flower experts sometimes refer to it), as well as its height when it's fully grown and the months when you might see it flowering.

Botanical name: *Viola riviniana*
Height: up to 15cm
When to spot: April–June

Common dog violet (page 38)

Parts of a plant

Wild flowers come in lots of different shapes and sizes, but they're all made up of the same basic parts that help them to grow, flower and scatter their seeds.

Seeds make new plants. They might be hidden in pods or fleshy fruits, or blow away on the breeze.

Flowers attract insects, such as bees, which spread pollen around as they fly from flower to flower. This pollinates the plant, which means that the seeds can start to develop.

Stems transport food and water around the plant.

Roots absorb water and minerals from the soil, as well as anchoring the plant in the ground.

Leaves use sunlight and water to make food, which helps the plant grow and stay healthy.

Where to spot wild flowers

Wild flowers grow in lots of different places. Each flower has a particular type of place where it grows best, though some are less picky than others. On the next few pages, you can find out about the main places to look for them.

Woodland

Woodlands are good places to find flowers. Try to go in spring, before the new leaves on the trees block out the light the flowers need. You might see beetles, birds and butterflies too, because they rely on the flowers for food and shelter.

Bluebell (page 24)

Common cow-wheat (page 14)

Red campion (page 34)

Wood anemone (page 56)

Meadows

Grassy fields and meadows are home to tall flowers that are often buzzing with insects. If you're in a meadow, it's important to follow the paths to avoid trampling on the plants.

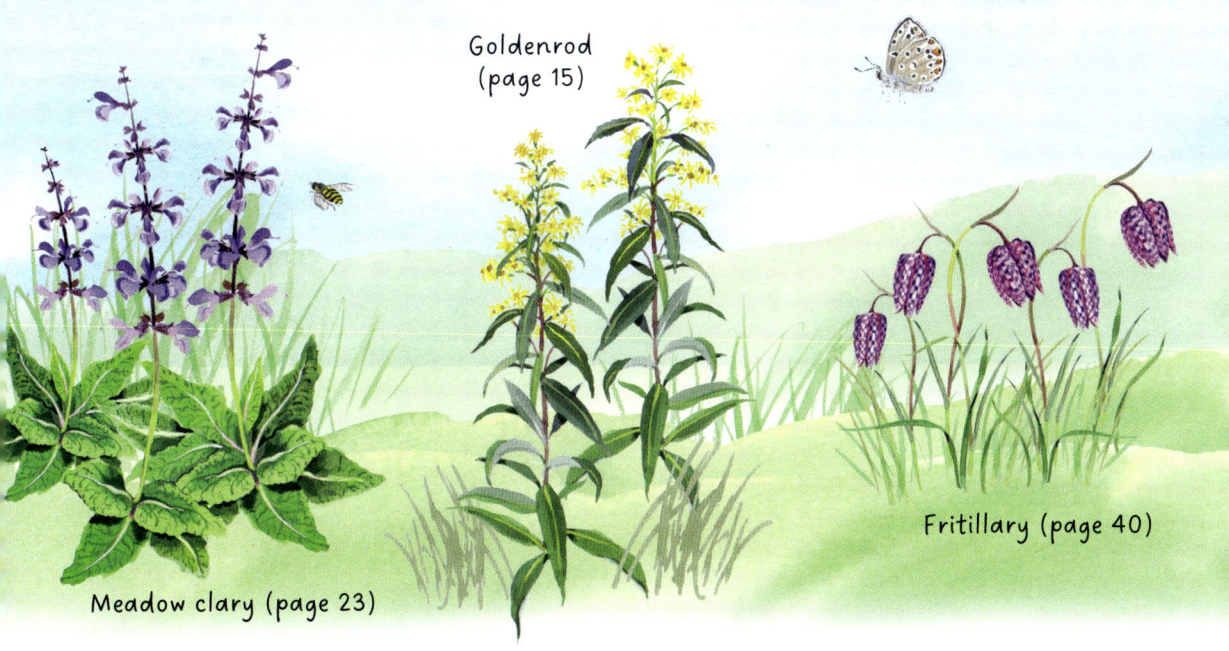

Goldenrod (page 15)

Fritillary (page 40)

Meadow clary (page 23)

Towns and cities

You might not expect to find flowers in the middle of a town... but keep your eyes open! Some plants actually prefer dry, rocky places. You might spot them popping up through cracks in the pavement, along railway lines and on wasteland.

Ivy-leaved toadflax (page 42)

Biting stonecrop (page 20)

Ragwort (page 12)

Rivers, streams and ponds

Every plant needs water to survive, but some are thirstier than others. Whether they're floating in a garden pond or lining a wide riverbank, you can spot water-loving wild flowers all summer long.

Brooklime (page 22)

Water crowfoot (page 48)

Purple loosestrife (page 43)

Yellow water lily (page 16)

Heaths and moors

Flowers in these wild, open landscapes need to be tough to cope with the wind that whips across them. If you want to see a spectacular sight, visit in autumn when the heather is in full bloom.

Gorse (page 21)

Wild thyme (page 34)

Heather (page 36)

On the coast

You can even spot wild flowers on a trip to the seaside, growing high up on cliffs and along the shore. Most plants would struggle in the salty, sandy soil, but some have adapted to live with it.

Yellow horned poppy (page 20)

Thrift (page 37)

Sea holly (page 26)

Yellow flowers

Dandelion

Its golden flowers turn into 'clocks' of fluffy seeds about two weeks after they bloom. Grows almost anywhere, anchored deep into the ground by a long, thick root.

Seeds blow away on the breeze

Botanical name: *Taraxacum officinale*
Height: up to 45cm
When to spot: April–September

Creeping cinquefoil

Each flower has five petals – 'cinq' means five in French. Spreads fast thanks to long shoots that 'creep' along the ground, then send new roots into the soil.

Flowers close at night and on cloudy days

Botanical name: *Potentilla reptans*
Height: up to 20cm
When to spot: June–September

Bird's-foot trefoil

Grows close to the ground in grassy places. Gets its name from its seed pods, which are curved and sharp like birds' claws.

Seed pod

Botanical name: *Lotus corniculatus*
Height: up to 20cm
When to spot: May–September

Coltsfoot

These bright flowers look a bit like small dandelions but have thick, scaly stems. The fuzzy leaves appear later in the year.

Botanical name: *Tussilago farfara*
Height: up to 30cm
When to spot: February–April

Fluffy seedheads

Droopy flowers

Cowslip

Nodding, pale yellow blossoms grow in clusters at the top of straight stems. You'll find this spring flower in grassy meadows.

Botanical name: *Primula veris*
Height: up to 25cm
When to spot: April–May

Thick, wrinkly leaves

Yellow-rattle

Little flowers that fade into brown, papery pods with small, hard seeds inside them. Try shaking the tall stems to hear them rattling.

Botanical name: *Rhinanthus minor*
Height: up to 50cm
When to spot: May–September

Seed pods

Yellow flowers

Groundsel

Growing along roadsides and on wasteland, this tough plant survives where most others can't. Rabbits and birds enjoy snacking on the seeds.

Botanical name: *Senecio vulgaris*
Height: up to 40cm
When to spot: January–December

Tube-shaped flower heads

Pineappleweed

Look out for its pineapple-shaped flower heads on rocky paths and pavements. Try squeezing one to catch a whiff of pineapple scent.

Botanical name: *Matricaria discoidea*
Height: up to 40cm
When to spot: May–November

Feathery leaves

Common toadflax

A tall plant that attracts bumblebees. Often called 'butter-and-eggs' because of its pale yellow and orange flowers.

Botanical name: *Linaria vulgaris*
Height: up to 75cm
When to spot: June–November

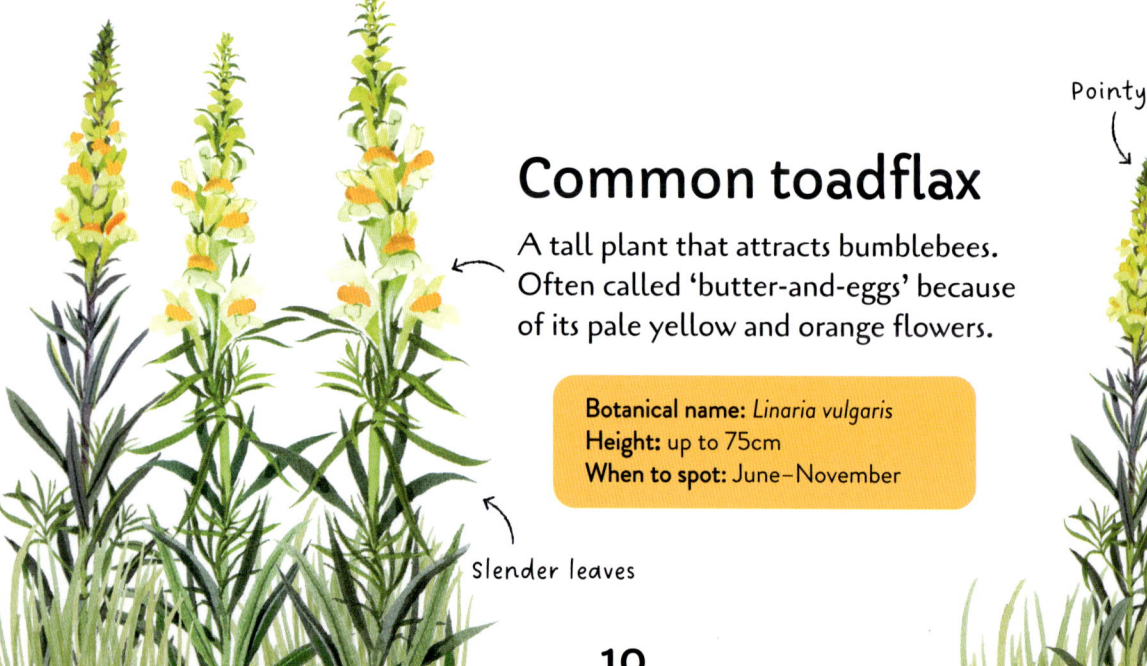
Pointy tip
Slender leaves

Silverweed

Small, bright flowers that glow against a bed of dark leaves. If you look underneath the leaves, you'll see that they're covered in fuzzy, silvery hairs.

Botanical name: *Potentilla anserina*
Height: up to 15cm
When to spot: June–August

Red runners help it spread

Looks a bit like a dandelion

Milky sap inside

Prickly sow-thistle

Can grow over a metre tall. Be careful not to prick your fingers on its thick, spiky leaves.

Botanical name: *Sonchus asper*
Height: up to 1.5m
When to spot: May–November

Lady's bedstraw

You might smell the sweet honey scent of this plant wafting across fields. In medieval times, people stuffed their mattresses with it.

Botanical name: *Galium verum*
Height: up to 30cm
When to spot: June–September

Rings of needle-shaped leaves

Yellow flowers

Field pansy

You can find these little flowers sprinkled across grassy meadows. Their creamy yellow petals sometimes have a pale purple tinge.

Botanical name: *Viola arvensis*
Height: up to 20cm
When to spot: April–October

Dark purple veins

Hairy leaves

Meadow buttercup

Glossy petals reflect the light

Common and easy to spot on a summer's day. The flowers are so glossy and bright that if you hold one under someone's chin, you might see a golden glow.

Botanical name: *Ranunculus acris*
Height: up to 1m
When to spot: April–October

Ragwort

Brightens up wasteland from summer to autumn with its bushy bunches. Caterpillars often munch on the leaves.

Botanical name: *Senecio jacobaea*
Height: up to 1.5m
When to spot: June–November

Wrinkly leaves

Wild daffodil

These flowers bloom in shady woodland at the start of spring. They're paler than the daffodils found in parks and gardens, and the inner trumpets are dark yellow.

Botanical name: *Narcissus pseudonarcissus*
Height: up to 35cm
When to spot: March–April

Pale outer petals

Slender leaves start at the bottom

Leaves are thick and fleshy

Opposite-leaved golden saxifrage

A leafy plant that grows low to the ground in patches of gold and green. Prefers damp soil, so you can often spot it near rivers and streams.

Botanical name: *Chrysosplenium oppositifolium*
Height: up to 15cm
When to spot: April–June

St. John's wort

Its star-shaped flowers have a musky smell. If you look closely at its leaves you'll see tiny, pale freckles all over them.

Botanical name: *Hypericum perforatum*
Height: up to 1m
When to spot: June–September

Star-shaped flowers

Clear dots on leaves

Yellow flowers

Common cow-wheat

Golden flowers that grow in pairs. Ants carry the seeds back to their nests, which creates large patches of cow-wheat within woodland.

Botanical name: *Melampyrum pratense*
Height: up to 50cm
When to spot: May–September

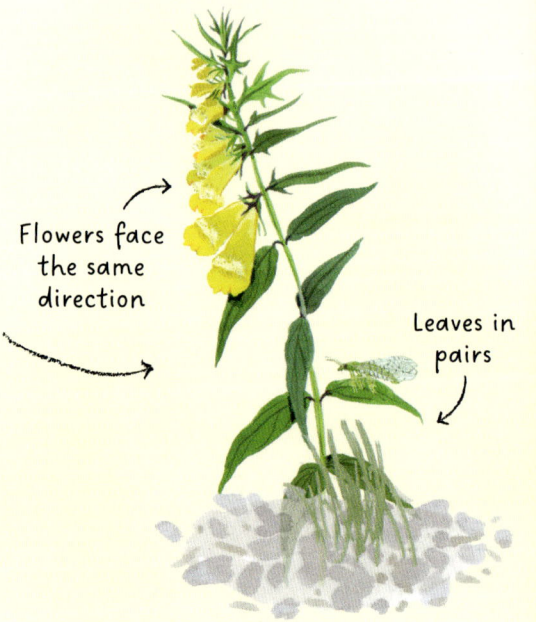

Flowers face the same direction

Leaves in pairs

Red stripes

Mouse-ear hawkweed

If you peep under its petals, you might find striking red stripes. White, fuzzy hairs cover its leaves and stem.

Botanical name: *Pilosella officinarum*
Height: up to 25cm
When to spot: May–October

Lemony scent when open

Common evening-primrose

As the air grows cooler and the sun begins to set, this plant slowly wakes up. If you watch it for a while, you might see its flowers opening.

Botanical name: *Oenothera biennis*
Height: up to 1.5m
When to spot: June–September

Common fleabane

A burst of bright petals found growing in marshy soil. The smoke from burning the plant is said to keep fleas away.

Botanical name: *Pulicaria dysenterica*
Height: up to 90cm
When to spot: July–September

Look like big yellow daisies

Large, wrinkly leaves

Feathery leaves

Tansy

Easy to spot by the small, round flower heads that give it the nickname 'golden buttons'. Try crushing one of the leaves – they smell herby.

Botanical name: *Tanacetum vulgare*
Height: up to 90cm
When to spot: July–October

Goldenrod

Standing tall in sunny meadows, this plant is a magnet for bees, butterflies and moths. Has small, bright flowers which can be used to make a yellow dye.

Botanical name: *Solidago virgaurea*
Height: up to 60cm
When to spot: July–September

Reddish stems

Yellow flowers

Bog asphodel

Star-shaped flowers that bloom in summer. During autumn, the stem and seedheads turn a rusty shade of orange.

Botanical name: *Narthecium ossifragum*
Height: up to 40cm
When to spot: June–August

Cluster of buds

Dark brown markings

Yellow flag iris

This thirsty plant grows along the sides of rivers and streams, where the water is shallow. Has leafy stems and droopy yellow petals.

Botanical name: *Iris pseudacorus*
Height: up to 1.5m
When to spot: May–August

Yellow water lily

Look out for flat lily pads floating in canals and ponds. Beneath the surface, long stems anchor them to the mud below.

Botanical name: *Nuphar lutea*
Height: up to 60cm (above the water)
When to spot: June–September

Dragonflies lay eggs on lily pads

Marsh-marigold

Commonly found around the edges of ponds, where its leaves provide shelter for frogs. Also known as 'kingcup' because its flowers are said to look like golden goblets.

Botanical name: *Caltha palustris*
Height: up to 50cm
When to spot: March–July

Five or six petals

Glossy like a buttercup

Shiny leaves

Lesser celandine

Keep an eye out for these flowers early in the year – they're one of the first to bloom. Thrives in damp, shady woodland.

Botanical name: *Ficaria verna*
Height: up to 25cm
When to spot: February–April

Yellow loosestrife

Sturdy stems covered in bright clusters of flowers. Often found in large clumps as it grows and spreads quickly.

Botanical name: *Lysimachia vulgaris*
Height: up to 1m
When to spot: June–September

Orange in the middle

Leaves are hairy

Yellow flowers

Wood avens

As the summer ends, these small flowers turn into spiky seedheads. They're covered in tiny hooks, which help them cling to animal fur.

Botanical name: *Geum urbanum*
Height: up to 50cm
When to spot: May–August

Hooks

Yellow pimpernel

Vivid yellow flowers found in damp soil. It has small leaves and sprawling stems, which help it to spread quickly.

Botanical name: *Lysimachia nemorum*
Height: up to 20cm
When to spot: May–August

Trails along the ground

Rounded star shape

Leaves look similar to a stinging nettle's

Yellow archangel

Mingling with bluebells, this plant thrives in woodland. Rings of bright flowers emerge from its rounded buds in late spring.

Botanical name: *Lamium galeobdolon*
Height: up to 60cm
When to spot: May–June

Primrose

Found low to the ground with wrinkly leaves and fuzzy stems. Its pale lemon petals brighten up shady spots from winter into spring.

Botanical name: *Primula vulgaris*
Height: up to 20cm
When to spot: December–May

Leaves grow at the bottom

Petals overlap

Hairy buds

Welsh poppy

Big golden flowers that attract bees. The petals have a crinkled texture, a bit like crepe paper.

Botanical name: *Meconopsis cambrica*
Height: up to 50cm
When to spot: June–August

Honeysuckle

Climbs up walls and over hedges. Moths and bees feed on its nectar, and small birds make nests in its branches. Has a strong, sweet scent.

Botanical name: *Lonicera periclymenum*
Height: up to 7m
When to spot: June–August

Pink tinge

Yellow flowers

Fleshy leaves cover the stems

Biting stonecrop

Covers large patches of ground with its sunny flowers, giving it the nickname 'golden moss'. It's tougher than most plants and can survive on little water.

Botanical name: *Sedum acre*
Height: up to 10cm
When to spot: May–July

Yellow horned poppy

If you visit the coast, look out for it on rocky beaches. Small birds snack on its seeds, but the plant is poisonous to people – so don't touch it.

Botanical name: *Glaucium flavum*
Height: up to 50cm
When to spot: June–September

Horn-shaped seed pods

Looks similar to gorse, but it isn't spiky

Seed pod

Broom

Tall and bushy, this plant really was once used to make brooms! You might catch its vanilla scent when walking across heathland.

Botanical name: *Cytisus scoparius*
Height: up to 2m
When to spot: April–June

Gorse

Spiky shrub that was once used to feed cattle and fuel fires. Listen for the pop of its seed pods, which burst open in hot weather.

> **Botanical name:** *Ulex europaeus*
> **Height:** up to 2.5m
> **When to spot:** January–June

Completely covered in sharp spines

Large buds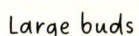

Golden samphire

Also known as sea samphire because it grows on salty cliffsides. Its leaves are thick and grow up towards the sky.

> **Botanical name:** *Limbarda crithmoides*
> **Height:** up to 1m
> **When to spot:** July–August

Thick leaves

Flowers are trumpet-shaped

Yellow corydalis

Pops up along walls and through cracks in pavements. Its small, trumpet-shaped flowers have an orange tinge.

> **Botanical name:** *Pseudofumaria lutea*
> **Height:** up to 40cm
> **When to spot:** May–October

Blue flowers

Leaves are shorter at the top

Cornflower

Look out for its bright blue and purple blooms in grassy meadows. It has pointy petals and small, hairy seeds.

Botanical name: *Centaurea cyanus*
Height: up to 80cm
When to spot: June–August

Brooklime

Found near streams and brooks, where tadpoles and small fish shelter under its broad leaves. Little flowers branch off the thick stems.

Botanical name: *Veronica beccabunga*
Height: up to 30cm
When to spot: May–September

Flowers white in middle

Scallop-edged leaves

Ground ivy

Clings low to damp soil and spreads quickly, giving it the nickname 'creeping Charlie'. Its delicate flowers are speckled with dark purple blotches.

Botanical name: *Glechoma hederacea*
Height: up to 50cm
When to spot: March–June

Green alkanet

A hairy plant that spreads rapidly. It has thick roots that burrow deep underground. You might spot its big, bristly leaves in shady places all year round.

Botanical name: *Pentaglottis sempervirens*
Height: up to 90cm
When to spot: March–September

Larkspur

Elegant spires studded with deep blue flowers that bloom in summer. Look at the flowers from the side to see the long, curved tail on each one.

Botanical name: *Consolida regalis*
Height: up to 60cm
When to spot: May–August

Meadow clary

Curved petals sit opposite each other like a pair of wings. It's now a rare sight, but you might still spot it in meadows and woodland.

Botanical name: *Salvia pratensis*
Height: up to 90cm
When to spot: June–August

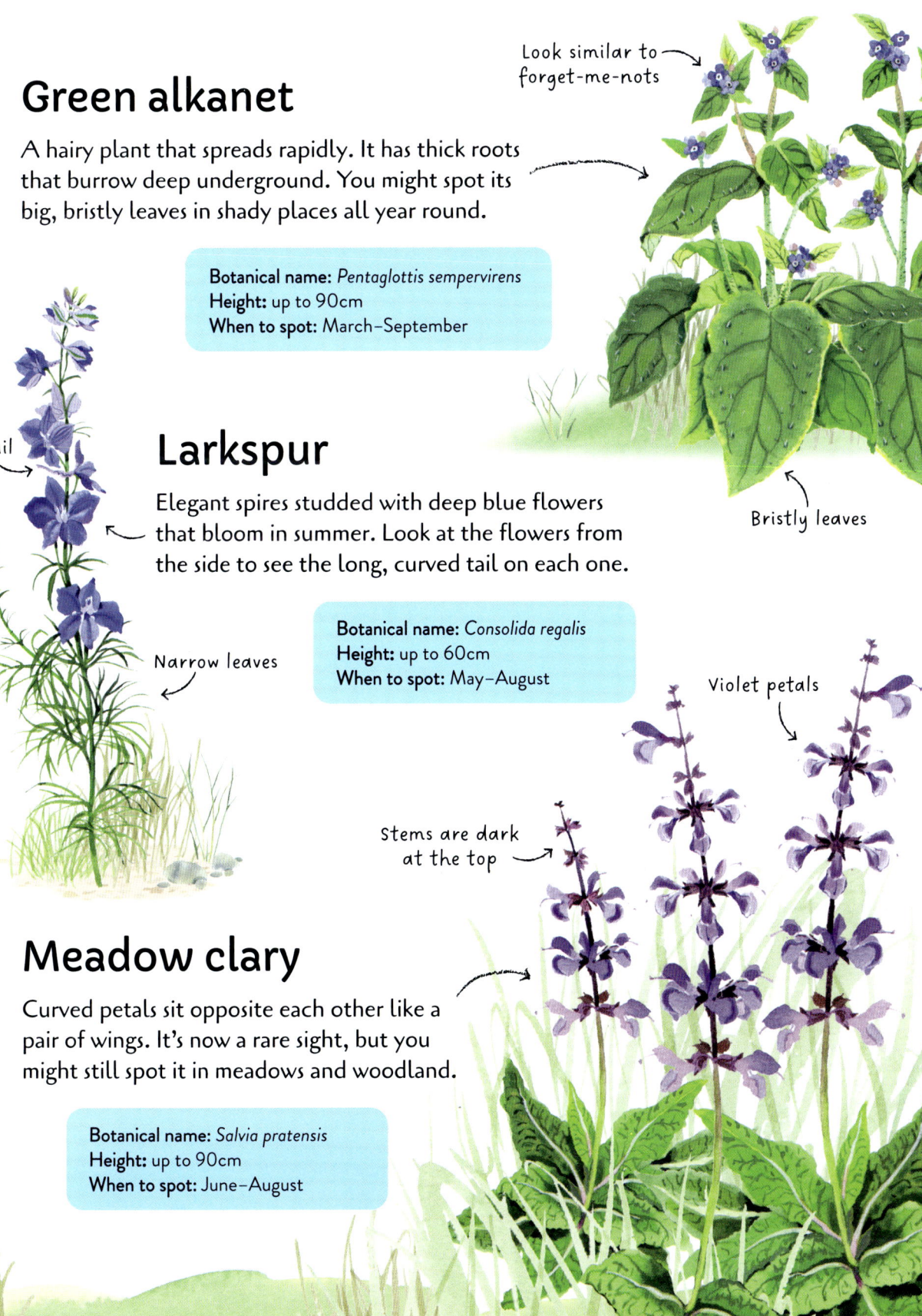

Blue flowers

Lesser periwinkle

Grows low down to the ground and spreads widely. Its pretty flowers have five flat petals and a purple tint.

> Botanical name: *Vinca minor*
> Height: up to 20cm
> When to spot: March–May

Glossy leaves

Forget-me-not

Bunches of sky-blue flowers that sway on hairy stems. Its leaves are long and narrow. A common sight in damp, shady places.

> Botanical name: *Myosotis sylvatica*
> Height: up to 30cm
> When to spot: April–June

White or yellow dot in the middle

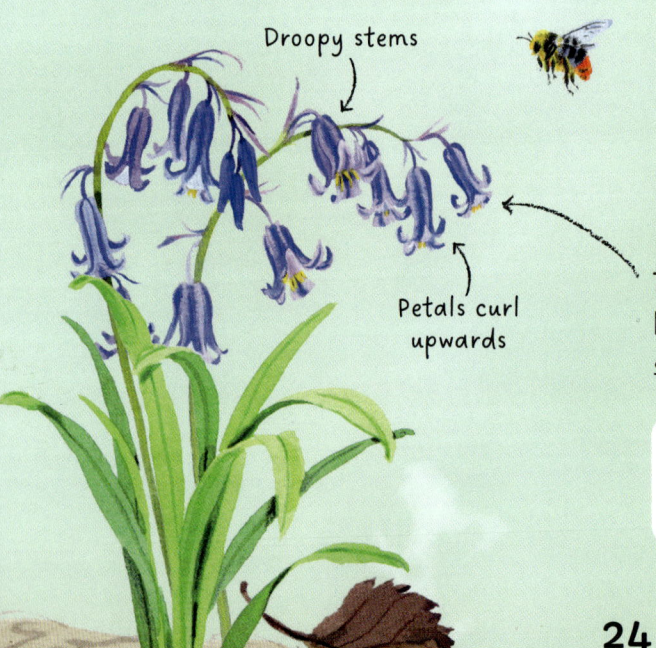

Droopy stems

Petals curl upwards

Bluebell

Transforms woodland into a sea of blue. Its bell-shaped flowers are a sure sign that spring has arrived.

> Botanical name: *Hyacinthoides non-scripta*
> Height: up to 50cm
> When to spot: April–May

Dainty stripes on petals

Germander speedwell

These little flowers grow along roadsides and country lanes. People used to think that they brought good luck to travellers.

Botanical name: *Veronica chamaedrys*
Height: up to 20cm
When to spot: April–June

Small, fuzzy leaves

Hairy stem

Bugle

Short, reddish stems and purple-tinged leaves give it the nickname 'burgundy glow'. Its nectar attracts white-tailed bumblebees.

Botanical name: *Ajuga reptans*
Height: up to 20cm
When to spot: April–July

Top petal of each flower is shaped like a hood

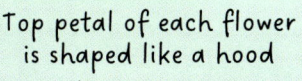

Monkshood

Pretty but poisonous – admire it from a distance but stay away. Gets its name from the shape of its flowers. Also known as 'wolfsbane'.

Botanical name: *Aconitum napellus*
Height: up to 1.5m
When to spot: May–September

Blue flowers

Sea holly

A striking, spiky plant that can be silvery grey or dazzling blue. You might spot it in the sand on a coastal walk.

Botanical name: *Eryngium maritimum*
Height: up to 60cm
When to spot: July–September

Sharp spines on leaves

Straight stem

Viper's bugloss

Hairy, speckled stems studded with vibrant flowers. Thrives in sunny spots near the sea, such as sand dunes and clifftops.

Botanical name: *Echium vulgare*
Height: up to 80cm
When to spot: May–September

Stem oozes a milky sap when broken

Harebell

Pale, bell-shaped flowers that nod on slender stems. In Scottish folklore, they're home to fairies and used in witches' spells.

Botanical name: *Campanula rotundifolia*
Height: up to 40cm
When to spot: July–September

Common sea-lavender

Clusters of delicate flowers that live by the seaside. Doesn't actually smell like lavender, as it belongs to a different plant family.

> **Botanical name:** *Limonium vulgare*
> **Height:** up to 30cm
> **When to spot:** July–October

Leaves only grow at the bottom

Slender stem

Covered in white hairs

Sheep's-bit

Its small blue flowers look like wild pom-poms. Sheep enjoy munching on them, as the name suggests.

> **Botanical name:** *Jasione montana*
> **Height:** up to 50cm
> **When to spot:** May–September

Ivy-leaved speedwell

Look for this plant trailing across the ground or sprawling along a wall. It has hairy leaves and small, stripy flowers.

> **Botanical name:** *Veronica hederifolia*
> **Height:** up to 50cm
> **When to spot:** March–August

Four petals

Pink flowers

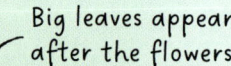
Big leaves appear after the flowers

Butterbur

Gets its name from its leaves, which can grow up to a metre wide and were once used to wrap butter. The cluster of pink flowers appears in early spring.

Botanical name: *Petasites hybridus*
Height: up to 40cm
When to spot: March–May

Herb Robert

Its small flowers attract many different butterflies. It has feathery leaves, and the stems turn red if it's growing in a sunny spot.

Pale white stripes

Stems turn red

Botanical name: *Geranium robertianum*
Height: up to 30cm
When to spot: May–September

Heart-shaped leaves

Bindweed

A climbing plant that can quickly smother other, slower-growing plants. Its funnel-shaped flowers often have pink and white stripes.

Can also be white

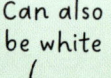

Botanical name: *Convolvulus arvensis*
Height: up to 2m
When to spot: June–September

Blackberry

Pale pink blossom that turns into fruit during summer. You can eat the sweet blackberries, but watch out for the sharp thorns. Also known as bramble.

Botanical name: *Rubus fruticosus*
Height: up to 3m
When to spot: May–September

Ready to eat when it turns black

Betony

Spikes of pinky-purple petals that top slender stems. In medieval times, people thought this plant could ward off evil spirits.

Botanical name: *Betonica officinalis*
Height: up to 60cm
When to spot: June–August

Rough, wrinkly leaves at the bottom

Enchanter's nightshade

Look out for these dainty flowers in shady woodland. The hairy seeds cling to animal fur, which helps the plant to spread widely.

Botanical name: *Circaea lutetiana*
Height: up to 70cm
When to spot: June–August

Dark red buds

29

Pink flowers

Bistort

Fluffy flowers that pop up along riverbanks. The wrinkly leaves used to be cooked with stinging nettles in a bitter dish called 'Easter ledge pudding'.

Botanical name: *Persicaria bistorta*
Height: up to 75cm
When to spot: June–August

Slender, upright stems

Pinky-white flowers

Soapwort

Its soft, sweet scent is strongest in the evening. Hundreds of years ago, people used this plant as a natural soap to wash their clothes.

Botanical name: *Saponaria officinalis*
Height: up to 70cm
When to spot: July–September

Himalayan balsam

One of the tallest wild flowers. Its large green seed pods burst open when they're ripe. Try gently pinching one to see it pop.

Botanical name: *Impatiens glandulifera*
Height: up to 2.5m
When to spot: July–October

Seed pods drop seeds into river

Jagged leaves

Marsh woundwort

If you look closely, you'll see dark purple blotches on the flowers. Used by the ancient Greeks to dress wounds and stop bleeding.

Botanical name: *Stachys palustris*
Height: up to 80cm
When to spot: June–September

Hairy buds

Dark flower buds

Ragged robin

A summer flower with large, frayed petals. Attracts bees, butterflies and moths, and thrives in marshy soil.

Botanical name: *Lychnis flos-cuculi*
Height: up to 75cm
When to spot: May–August

Cluster of leaves at the bottom

Hemp agrimony

Nicknamed 'raspberries and cream' because of its fluffy pink and white clusters. A tall and bushy plant that prefers damp soil.

Botanical name: *Eupatorium cannabinum*
Height: up to 1.5m
When to spot: July–September

Covered in soft hairs

Pink flowers

Common knapweed

A tough plant topped with a mop of pink petals. Looks a bit like a spear thistle, but it's hairy rather than spiky.

Botanical name: *Centaurea nigra*
Height: up to 1m
When to spot: June–September

Large bud

Shiny leaves at the bottom of the plant

Sorrel

The heart-shaped petals turn red when it's sunny. Often found growing alongside country roads.

Botanical name: *Rumex acetosa*
Height: up to 1m
When to spot: May–June

Centaury

Star-shaped flowers that bloom in bright sunshine and close in the afternoon. Grows in dry, sandy spots.

Botanical name: *Centaurium erythraea*
Height: up to 25cm
When to spot: June–September

Five petals

Rosebay willowherb

Sometimes called 'bombweed' because it spread rapidly in craters and ruins after the two World Wars. The hairy seeds make the plant look fluffy during autumn.

Botanical name: *Chamerion angustifolium*
Height: up to 1.5m
When to spot: June–September

Flowers at the bottom open first

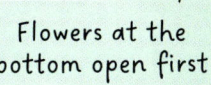

Dark red tips

Common fumitory

Tube-shaped flowers with dark red tips. Birds enjoy snacking on the hard, round seeds. Often grows in fields used for farming.

Botanical name: *Fumaria officinalis*
Height: up to 40cm
When to spot: April–October

Grey-green leaves

Red clover

Look out for patches of pink scattered in fields. The leaves are usually made up of three 'leaflets', but if you're really lucky you might spot one with four.

Botanical name: *Trifolium pratense*
Height: up to 40cm
When to spot: May–October

Known as a four-leaf clover

Pink flowers

Dark buds

Wild thyme

Grows in dense, dark patches up mountains and on rocky ground. If you brush against its leaves you'll smell a strong, herby scent.

Botanical name: *Thymus serpyllum*
Height: up to 5cm
When to spot: June–September

Red campion

Brightens woodland after the bluebells have finished blooming. Its dark, round seeds were once thought to cure snake bites.

Botanical name: *Silene dioica*
Height: up to 1m
When to spot: May–September

Petals have two tips

Pinky-purple flowers

Common mallow

Keep an eye out for its stripy petals along roadsides and on wasteland. The leaves have a mild, nutty taste and were eaten by the ancient Romans.

Botanical name: *Malva sylvestris*
Height: up to 1.5m
When to spot: June–October

Dog rose

Pink flowers that turn into shiny, red fruit called rosehips. The stems are covered in prickles, which help it to climb up other plants.

Botanical name: *Rosa canina*
Height: up to 4m
When to spot: June–July

Five petals

Rosehips are eaten by birds

Pale, veiny flowers

Lady's smock

Said to appear when the cuckoos first call in spring. It has unusual leaves that are round at the bottom of the stem, but long and thin further up.

Botanical name: *Cardamine pratensis*
Height: up to 50cm
When to spot: April–June

Water mint

Its hairy leaves can have a purple tint. If you crush one in your fingers you'll notice a fresh, minty smell. Grows in damp places, where it attracts butterflies and beetles.

Botanical name: *Mentha aquatica*
Height: up to 50cm
When to spot: July–October

Flower clusters grow up the stems

Wrinkly leaves

Pink flowers

Heather

If you go for a walk across the moors you'll be sure to see this shrub. In autumn, it transforms the ragged landscape with thousands of tiny, pink flowers. Also known as ling.

Botanical name: *Calluna vulgaris*
Height: up to 60cm
When to spot: August–October

← Brown, twiggy stems

Bell heather

Clusters of vibrant, bell-shaped blooms. Visiting bumblebees make a dark, fragrant honey from its nectar.

Botanical name: *Erica cinerea*
Height: up to 50cm
When to spot: July–September

Flowers are more close than heather

Knotgrass

Creeps along grassy ground, spreading far and wide. You'll have to look closely to see the flowers, which sprout directly from its stems.

Botanical name: *Polygonum aviculare*
Height: up to 60cm
When to spot: May–October

← Tiny flowers

Sea aster

Cheerful bunches of pale blooms dotted along the coast. In autumn, the seedheads look a bit like dandelion 'clocks'.

Botanical name: *Tripolium pannonicum*
Height: up to 50cm
When to spot: July–September

Look similar to daisies

Lots of little flowers bunched together

Slender leaves

Thrift

Also known as 'sea pink', you'll find it on pebbly beaches and clifftops. A pretty plant but a tough one too – it doesn't need much water to survive.

Botanical name: *Armeria maritima*
Height: up to 20cm
When to spot: April–July

Bilberry

In late summer, its reddish flowers turn into tiny, tart berries that look a bit like blueberries. They can be cooked to make pies and jams.

Botanical name: *Vaccinium myrtillus*
Height: up to 50cm
When to spot: April–June

Pinkish-red inside

Purple flowers

Jagged leaves

Bats-in-the-belfry

A hairy plant with bell-shaped flowers that can be pale or dark purple. Has large, jagged leaves, and grows in shady woodland.

Botanical name: *Campanula trachelium*
Height: up to 90cm
When to spot: July–September

Common dog violet

Look close to the ground to find these little flowers. They have a stripy petal pattern and heart-shaped leaves.

Botanical name: *Viola riviniana*
Height: up to 15cm
When to spot: April–June

Stripes

Leaves are dark green

Common spotted orchid

Gets its name from the dark spots on its leaves. A striking sight when the pale flowers burst into bloom during summer.

Cone of flowers

Botanical name: *Dactylorhiza fuchsii*
Height: up to 60cm
When to spot: June–August

Columbine

Its dark, droopy flowers have an inner and outer layer of frilly petals which give it the nickname 'granny's bonnet'. Grows in damp woodland.

Botanical name: *Aquilegia vulgaris*
Height: up to 1m
When to spot: May–June

Stems are reddish

Tufted vetch

Latches onto other plants by twisting its curly tendrils around them. Its seed pods, which look like little pea pods, turn dark brown when they're ripe.

Botanical name: *Vicia cracca*
Height: up to 2m
When to spot: June–August

Droopy stems

Tendrils

Foxglove

These tall spikes are a common summer sight, but they are known for their poison. If you spot them, make sure you don't touch them.

Botanical name: *Digitalis purpurea*
Height: up to 2m
When to spot: June–September

Pointy tip

Dark spots inside flowers

Purple flowers

Field scabious

Bright purple flowers that turn into fuzzy, green seedheads. Grows in damp places, where many bees and butterflies feed on its nectar.

Looks similar to a cornflower

Botanical name: *Knautia arvensis*
Height: up to 1.5m
When to spot: July–October

Said to look like a snake's head

Slender leaves

Fritillary

These unusual-looking flowers are a rare sight, but you might see them in wet meadows. Their reddish-purple petals have an intricate chequered pattern.

Botanical name: *Fritillaria meleagris*
Height: up to 30cm
When to spot: April–May

Spear thistle

This tough plant is known for its sharp spines. It has fluffy flower heads, and the seeds are white and wispy like a dandelion's.

Botanical name: *Cirsium vulgare*
Height: up to 1m
When to spot: July–October

Sharp spines

Teasel

Rings of tiny purple flowers sit around the spiky flower heads. They turn brown and bristly in winter, covered in sharp prickles like little hedgehogs.

Botanical name: *Dipsacus fullonum*
Height: up to 2m
When to spot: July–August

Seedhead in winter

Sharp spines

A bur covered in hooks

Greater burdock

The tiny hooks on its burs latch onto fabric and fur, which is how it spreads its seeds. If you gently brush one against your clothes, you'll find that it really sticks!

Botanical name: *Arctium lappa*
Height: up to 2m
When to spot: July–September

Purple tuft at the top

Meadow cranesbill

Veiny, violet flowers and feathery leaves. Named after its beak-like seed pods, which burst to disperse their seeds.

Botanical name: *Geranium pratense*
Height: up to 90cm
When to spot: June–September

Seed pod

Purple flowers

Early purple orchid

Its glossy leaves are covered in dark, uneven splotches that look like drops of ink. The top of the stem is purple and can hold up to 50 vibrant flowers.

> **Botanical name:** *Orchis mascula*
> **Height:** up to 40cm
> **When to spot:** April–June

Spots inside flowers

Dark splotches

Purple toadflax

A tall, bushy plant with slender leaves and a cone of flowers. Its roots grow deep, fixing it firmly in the ground. You might also be able to spot yellow toadflax.

> **Botanical name:** *Linaria purpurea*
> **Height:** up to 75cm
> **When to spot:** July–October

Two petals per flower

Pointy tip

Ivy-leaved toadflax

You can find these little lilac flowers sprinkled in rocky places. They cling to the surface and drop their seeds into cracks and crevices.

Red runners help the plant cling on

> **Botanical name:** *Cymbalaria muralis*
> **Height:** up to 10cm
> **When to spot:** May–September

Common comfrey

Grows in damp soil near rivers and streams. Loved by gardeners because its leaves can help lure slugs away from other plants.

Botanical name: *Symphytum officinale*
Height: up to 1.5m
When to spot: May–June

Large and wrinkly

Petals are covered in tiny white hairs

Selfheal

Short stems topped with red and purple flower clusters. Has a long history of being used in medicine, from reducing fevers to treating burns.

Botanical name: *Prunella vulgaris*
Height: up to 30cm
When to spot: June–October

Often green at the tip

Purple loosestrife

These tall, bright spikes line riverbanks all summer long. Grows in large clumps, using its roots to spread quickly.

Botanical name: *Lythrum salicaria*
Height: up to 1.5m
When to spot: June–August

Red and orange flowers

Pheasant's eye

A rare summer flower with vivid, glossy petals that shine in the sun. Said to look like the black and yellow eye of a pheasant, with the red feathers around it.

Feathery leaves

> Botanical name: *Adonis annua*
> Height: up to 40cm
> When to spot: June–August

Flowers open in bright sunshine

Scarlet pimpernel

Nicknamed 'shepherd's weather-glass' because they close up on cloudy days. They're often more orange than scarlet, and can sometimes even be bright blue.

> Botanical name: *Anagallis arvensis*
> Height: up to 30cm
> When to spot: June–September

Seed pod

Common poppy

Vibrant flowers that filled empty battlefields after World War One, becoming a symbol of remembrance in the UK. The large green seed pods are full of tiny black seeds.

Papery petals

> Botanical name: *Papaver rhoeas*
> Height: up to 80cm
> When to spot: June–August

Fox-and-cubs

A fuzzy little plant with fine white hairs on its leaves and stems. Its dark buds are huddled underneath the orange flowers, a bit like a fox and her young cubs.

Botanical name: *Pilosella aurantiaca*
Height: up to 30cm
When to spot: June–September

Dark buds

Leaves sit flat against the ground

Hedge woundwort

Has an unpleasant, musty smell that's strongest when the leaves are crushed. The reddish-purple flowers attract honeybees.

Botanical name: *Stachys sylvatica*
Height: up to 80cm
When to spot: June–October

Stem and leaves can have a purple tinge

Red valerian

Thrives in rocky places, from up on clifftops to along garden walls. Moths and butterflies drink its nectar.

Botanical name: *Centranthus ruber*
Height: up to 1m
When to spot: May–October

Teardrop-shaped leaves

White flowers

Garlic mustard

Nettle-like leaves that smell of garlic when crushed. It's common in shady places, and takes two years to flower.

Leaves smell of garlic

Botanical name: *Alliaria petiolata*
Height: up to 1m
When to spot: April–June

Blossom appears before the berries

Unripe berries are green

Wild strawberry

Small berries that turn juicy and red as they ripen. Their sweet taste is enjoyed by mice, slugs and birds – as well as people! Has long runners that help it spread.

Botanical name: *Fragaria vesca*
Height: up to 30cm
When to spot: April–July

Tendrils look like springs

White bryony

A poisonous plant with green-tinged flowers and curly, coiling tendrils. Can grow very tall as it twines around other plants for support.

Botanical name: *Bryonia dioica*
Height: up to 4m
When to spot: May–August

Shepherd's purse

Heart-shaped seed pods branch off the slender stems. A single plant can make thousands of seeds, and the flowers can bloom at any time of year.

Botanical name: *Capsella bursa-pastoris*
Height: up to 40cm
When to spot: January–December

Seed pod

Flowers can have a purple tint

Wild angelica

You might spot its round, fluffy flower clusters in damp woodland. Has thick, sturdy stems that can be green or purple.

Botanical name: *Angelica sylvestris*
Height: up to 2m
When to spot: July–September

Cow parsley

Grows rapidly, lining country lanes with delicate flowers that give it the nickname 'lady's lace'. Prefers shady spots.

Botanical name: *Anthriscus sylvestris*
Height: up to 1m
When to spot: May–June

Feathery leaves

White flowers

Water plantain

Keep an eye out for its slender stems and large leaves poking out of shallow water. Flies often use the leaves as a place to rest.

Flowers can have a pink tinge

Botanical name: *Alisma plantago-aquatica*
Height: up to 1m
When to spot: June–September

Five petals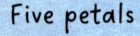

Water crowfoot

Anchored by long roots, this plant drifts and sways in the water. It spreads widely, and can cover streams and rivers like a flowery green carpet.

Botanical name: *Ranunculus aquatilis*
Height: up to 10cm (above the water)
When to spot: May–September

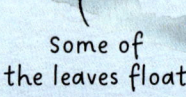
Some of the leaves float

Water soldier

Looks a bit like the top of a pineapple. A spiky plant that peeks above the surface to flower, then sinks back down when summer is over.

Only one flower per plant

Botanical name: *Stratiotes aloides*
Height: up to 15cm (above the water)
When to spot: June–August

Frogbit

Its round leaves look like a white water lily's but are much smaller. Grows in slow-moving water, such as ponds and canals.

> **Botanical name:** *Hydrocharis morsus-ranae*
> **Height:** up to 5cm (above the water)
> **When to spot:** July–August

Three crinkly petals

Flowers close in the afternoon

White water lily

These elegant flowers are the largest in the UK. Look out for broad, waxy lily pads that float on the surface and glisten in the sunshine.

> **Botanical name:** *Nymphaea alba*
> **Height:** up to 10cm (above the water)
> **When to spot:** June–August

Up to 30cm wide

Four petals

Watercress

Sits in streams or along muddy banks. You might have eaten farm-grown watercress in salads or sandwiches – the leaflets have a peppery taste.

> **Botanical name:** *Rorippa nasturtium-aquaticum*
> **Height:** up to 60cm
> **When to spot:** May–October

Leaflets

White flowers

Three-cornered leek

Known by the nickname 'stinking onion' – try crushing a leaf and you'll see why. Has a triangular stem, and grows from a small, white bulb, like a spring onion.

> **Botanical name:** *Allium triquetrum*
> **Height:** up to 40cm
> **When to spot:** April–June

Green stripes inside

Smells like onions when crushed

Meadowsweet

Its red stems line riverbanks during summer. Was once commonly used in wedding bouquets for its sweet smell and delicate, creamy flowers.

> **Botanical name:** *Filipendula ulmaria*
> **Height:** up to 1.2m
> **When to spot:** June–September

Red stem

Lesser water-parsnip

Scattered in ditches and damp places, it has dainty flowers that form umbrella shapes, known as 'umbels'. Smells like parsnips when the leaves are crumpled.

> **Botanical name:** *Berula erecta*
> **Height:** up to 1m
> **When to spot:** July–September

Umbel

Starry saxifrage

Star-shaped flowers with two yellow dots on each petal. Found nestled in rocky spots, with a clump of leaves at the bottom of its red stems.

Botanical name: *Saxifraga stellaris*
Height: up to 20cm
When to spot: June–August

Pink in the middle

Veiny flowers

Fairy flax

Often has droopy stems, even though the flowers are only small. In English folklore, it was said that fairies spun this plant to make their clothes.

Botanical name: *Linum catharticum*
Height: up to 30cm
When to spot: May–September

Pairs of leaves

Leaves can turn red in autumn

Gypsywort

You might have to take a close look at the stem before you notice the flowers. The sap of this plant was once used to dye clothes, and sometimes even skin.

Botanical name: *Lycopus europaeus*
Height: up to 80cm
When to spot: June–September

White flowers

Up to 20cm wide

Common hogweed

This plant is a magnet for all kinds of insects, but hogweed can be poisonous, so you should stay away. In autumn, the flowers turn into bundles of brown, papery seeds.

Botanical name: *Heracleum sphondylium*
Height: up to 2m
When to spot: May–August

Pink tinge

Hairy stem

Daisy

Look out for daisies in fields, parks and gardens – they're common in grassy places. They bloom all through the year and can sometimes have a pink tinge.

Botanical name: *Bellis perennis*
Height: up to 10cm
When to spot: January–December

Looks similar to common hogweed

Wild carrot

Gets its name from the carrot-like smell of its roots and leaves. Sometimes, a single red flower grows in the middle, which helps to attract insects.

Botanical name: *Daucus carota*
Height: up to 80cm
When to spot: June–September

White clover

You'll find this plant sprinkled across parks and fields. It grows low to the ground and is nibbled by deer and wood mice.

Botanical name: *Trifolium repens*
Height: up to 40cm
When to spot: May–October

Pale markings in a 'v' shape

Common mouse-ear

Has heart-shaped petals and hairy leaves that sit in pairs, like little mouse ears. Grows almost anywhere.

Botanical name: *Cerastium fontanum*
Height: up to 30cm
When to spot: April–September

White hairs on leaves

Yellow spot

Leaves can have purple edges

Eyebright

Small flowers with dark purple veins and yellow spots in the middle. In ancient Greek mythology, this plant could restore people's eyesight.

Botanical name: *Euphrasia officinalis*
Height: up to 25cm
When to spot: May–September

White flowers

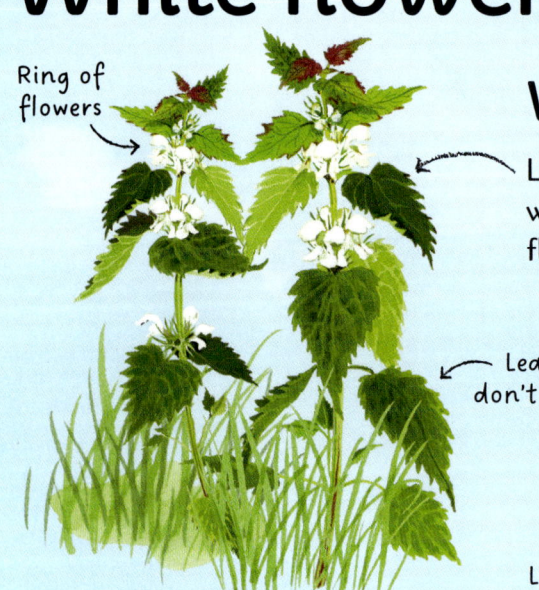

Ring of flowers

Leaves don't sting

White dead-nettle

Looks like a stinging nettle, but its leaves won't hurt you. A hairy plant with pale flowers that attract bumblebees.

Botanical name: *Lamium album*
Height: up to 80cm
When to spot: March–December

Petals have two tips

Large buds, often purplish

White campion

Every evening this pretty plant releases a soft scent that attracts night-flying moths. If it grows near red campion, they can mix together to make pinky-white flowers.

Botanical name: *Silene latifolia*
Height: up to 1m
When to spot: May–October

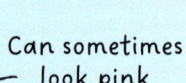

Can sometimes look pink

Yarrow

Has lots of fine, feathery leaves. The story goes that Achilles, the ancient Greek hero, treated his wounded soldiers on the battlefield with this plant.

Botanical name: *Achillea millefolium*
Height: up to 60cm
When to spot: June–November

Traveller's joy

A straggly climbing plant that weaves its way up hedges. During autumn, its flowers turn into fluffy seedheads, which give it the nickname 'old man's beard'.

Botanical name: *Clematis vitalba*
Height: up to 30m
When to spot: July–August

Covered in white hairs

Four petals

Up to 5cm wide

Ox-eye daisy

You can spot these big bright blooms growing along roadsides and on wasteland. The slim stems are often covered in dark red ridges.

Botanical name: *Leucanthemum vulgare*
Height: up to 60cm
When to spot: May–September

Droopy stems

Snowdrop

These early bloomers brighten the dark winter months. Each year their pale, drooping heads are a sign that spring is on its way.

Green markings

Botanical name: *Galanthus nivalis*
Height: up to 15cm
When to spot: January–March

White flowers

Crinkly petals

Wood anemone

Look for these flowers tucked close to the ground on a fresh spring day. Grows in clumps but spreads very slowly, getting only a few centimetres wider each year.

Botanical name: *Anemone nemorosa*
Height: up to 20cm
When to spot: March–May

Greater stitchwort

Listen out for the pop of its seed pods in late spring. Some people used to believe that picking this plant would trigger a thunderstorm.

Botanical name: *Stellaria holostea*
Height: up to 50cm
When to spot: April–June

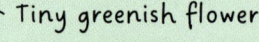

Stems break easily

Tiny greenish flowers

Leaves last all year round

Dog's mercury

A leafy plant with an unpleasant smell. Snails, beetles and crickets can eat the leaves, but you should stay away – they're poisonous to people.

Botanical name: *Mercurialis perennis*
Height: up to 35cm
When to spot: February–April

Lily of the valley

Dainty but dangerous, every part of this plant is poisonous. The white bells turn into bright bunches of red berries in autumn.

Thick leaves

Botanical name: *Convallaria majalis*
Height: up to 25cm
When to spot: May–June

Pointy petals

Long leaves at the bottom

Wild garlic

Fills woodland with a strong garlic smell – try following your nose and you might stumble upon a carpet of it. The leaves can be added to things like butter and soup.

Botanical name: *Allium ursinum*
Height: up to 35cm
When to spot: April–May

Purple veins

Flowers open in the sunshine

Wood sorrel

Grows in damp, mossy spots such as tree stumps and fallen logs. As the light fades, its little leaves fold in on themselves. The flowers close too, drooping as they do.

Botanical name: *Oxalis acetosella*
Height: up to 10cm
When to spot: April–May

Green and brown flowers

Ribwort plantain

Slender stems topped with dark flower heads. Rabbits sometimes nibble on the long leaves that grow around the bottom, and birds eat the seeds during winter.

Botanical name: *Plantago lanceolata*
Height: up to 50cm
When to spot: April–October

Ring of pollen

Flower spike

Greater plantain

A tough little plant that thrives on rough ground, sprouting up along paths and pavements. Its long, scaly flower spikes give it the nickname 'rat's tail'.

Botanical name: *Plantago major*
Height: up to 20cm
When to spot: June–October

Broad, flat leaves

Seed pods

Common orache

Has small, reddish flowers and fleshy seed pods. The leaves have a grainy texture, as though they've been sprinkled with salt.

Botanical name: *Atriplex patula*
Height: up to 80cm
When to spot: July–October

Pellitory-of-the-wall

You might find it clinging to the cracks of old stone ruins or growing inside a damp cave. The whole plant, including its flowers, is covered in white hairs.

Botanical name: *Parietaria judaica*
Height: up to 70cm
When to spot: June–October

Red stems

Pink-tipped flowers

Annual meadow grass

This short, ragged grass thrives in fields and farmland, flowering all year round. A seed can become a fully-grown plant in just six weeks.

Botanical name: *Poa annua*
Height: up to 25cm
When to spot: January–December

Tassels of tiny flowers

Covered in sharp hairs

Stinging nettle

Be careful not to brush against these when you're out on a walk. Their painful sting (caused by tiny, needle-sharp hairs) can leave red, itchy bumps on your skin.

Botanical name: *Urtica dioica*
Height: up to 1.5m
When to spot: May–September

Green and brown flowers

Good King Henry

Its large, frilly leaves have been cooked and eaten for hundreds of years. The older the leaf is, the more bitter it tastes.

Pointy tip

> Botanical name: *Blitum bonus-henricus*
> Height: up to 80cm
> When to spot: May–July

Heart-shaped leaves

Cuckoo-pint

A mysterious, poisonous flower that turns into a striking spike of red berries during autumn. Has a strong, foul smell that attracts flies.

Only birds can eat the berries

> Botanical name: *Arum maculatum*
> Height: up to 50cm
> When to spot: April–May

Berries are green before they're ripe

Ivy

You'll be able to spot its glossy leaves all year, wrapped around tree trunks and covering walls. During winter, its green flowers turn into handfuls of dark, poisonous berries.

> Botanical name: *Hedera helix*
> Height: up to 30m
> When to spot: September–November

Marsh samphire

Look out for these gnarled, green shoots popping out of the mud along seafronts. The stems can be cooked in butter and added to fish dishes for a salty crunch.

Split into segments

> **Botanical name:** *Salicornia europaea*
> **Height:** up to 30cm
> **When to spot:** August–September

Flowers turn dark red

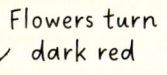

Broad-leaved dock

If you get stung by a nettle, some people believe that rubbing a dock leaf on the rash will help soothe the pain. Scientists aren't sure if it actually works – but it's worth a try!

> **Botanical name:** *Rumex obtusifolius*
> **Height:** up to 1m
> **When to spot:** June–October

Leaves can have red veins

Goosegrass

Also called 'sticky weed', it's covered in tiny hooks that cling to clothes and animal fur. Sprawls along the ground, climbing over other plants.

Four petals

> **Botanical name:** *Galium aparine*
> **Height:** up to 1.5m
> **When to spot:** May–August

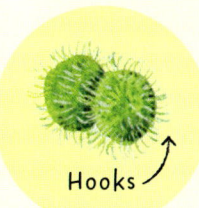

Hooks

Wild flower calendar

Not every wild flower waits until spring or summer to bloom. You can use this calendar to see some of the flowers you might spot during different seasons.

Winter

Snowdrop	Primrose	Daisy
Lesser celandine	Gorse	Shepherd's purse

Spring

Wild daffodil	Lesser periwinkle	Ivy-leaved speedwell
Dandelion	Bluebell	Fritillary
Broom	Forget-me-not	Meadow buttercup
Field pansy	Lily of the valley	Cow parsley

Summer

Pheasant's eye	Starry saxifrage	Meadow cranesbill
White water lily	Dog rose	Common poppy
Cornflower	Foxglove	Lady's bedstraw
Harebell	Sea holly	Himalayan balsam
Common toadflax	Sea aster	Spear thistle

Autumn

White clover	Yellow corydalis	Bindweed
Ragwort	Yarrow	Ivy

Index

Annual meadow grass 59

Bats-in-the-belfry 38
Bell heather 36
Betony 29
Bilberry 37
Bindweed 28
Bird's-foot trefoil 8
Bistort 30
Biting stonecrop 20
Blackberry 29
Bluebell 24
Bog asphodel 16
Broad-leaved dock 61
Brooklime 22
Broom 20
Bugle 25
Butterbur 28

Centaury 32
Coltsfoot 9
Columbine 39
Common comfrey 43
Common cow-wheat 14
Common dog violet 38
Common evening-primrose 14
Common fleabane 15
Common fumitory 33
Common hogweed 52
Common knapweed 32
Common mallow 34
Common mouse-ear 53
Common orache 58
Common poppy 44
Common sea-lavender 27
Common spotted orchid 38
Common toadflax 10
Cornflower 22
Cow parsley 47
Cowslip 9
Creeping cinquefoil 8
Cuckoo-pint 60

Daisy 52
Dandelion 8
Dog rose 35

Dog's mercury 56

Early purple orchid 42
Enchanter's nightshade 29
Eyebright 53

Fairy flax 51
Field pansy 12
Field scabious 40
Forget-me-not 24
Fox-and-cubs 45
Foxglove 39
Fritillary 40
Frogbit 49

Garlic mustard 46
Germander speedwell 25
Golden samphire 21
Goldenrod 15
Good King Henry 60
Goosegrass 61
Gorse 21
Greater burdock 41
Greater plantain 58
Greater stitchwort 56
Green alkanet 23
Ground ivy 22
Groundsel 10
Gypsywort 51

Harebell 26
Heather 36
Hedge woundwort 45
Hemp agrimony 31
Herb Robert 28
Himalayan balsam 30
Honeysuckle 19

Ivy 60
Ivy-leaved speedwell 27
Ivy-leaved toadflax 42

Knotgrass 36

Lady's bedstraw 11
Lady's smock 35

Larkspur 23
Lesser celandine 17
Lesser periwinkle 24
Lesser water-parsnip 50
Lily of the valley 57

Marsh samphire 61
Marsh woundwort 31
Marsh-marigold 17
Meadow buttercup 12
Meadow clary 23
Meadow cranesbill 41
Meadowsweet 50
Monkshood 25
Mouse-ear hawkweed 14

Opposite-leaved
  golden saxifrage 13
Ox-eye daisy 55

Pellitory-of-the-wall 59
Pheasant's eye 44
Pineappleweed 10
Prickly sow-thistle 11
Primrose 19
Purple loosestrife 43
Purple toadflax 42

Ragged robin 31
Ragwort 12
Red campion 34
Red clover 33
Red valerian 45
Ribwort plantain 58
Rosebay willowherb 33

Scarlet pimpernel 44
Sea aster 37
Sea holly 26
Selfheal 43
Sheep's-bit 27
Shepherd's purse 47
Silverweed 11
Snowdrop 55
Soapwort 30
Sorrel 32

Spear thistle 40
Starry saxifrage 51
Stinging nettle 59
St. John's wort 13

Tansy 15
Teasel 41
Three-cornered leek 50
Thrift 37
Traveller's joy 55
Tufted vetch 39

Viper's bugloss 26

Water crowfoot 48
Water mint 35
Water plantain 48
Water soldier 48
Watercress 49
Welsh poppy 19
White bryony 46
White campion 54
White clover 53
White dead-nettle 54
White water lily 49
Wild angelica 47
Wild carrot 52
Wild daffodil 13
Wild garlic 57
Wild strawberry 46
Wild thyme 34
Wood anemone 56
Wood avens 18
Wood sorrel 57

Yarrow 54
Yellow archangel 18
Yellow corydalis 21
Yellow flag iris 16
Yellow horned poppy 20
Yellow loosestrife 17
Yellow pimpernel 18
Yellow water lily 16
Yellow-rattle 9

First published in 2025 by Usborne Publishing Limited, 83–85 Saffron Hill, London EC1N 8RT, United Kingdom. usborne.com
Copyright © 2025 Usborne Publishing Limited. The name Usborne and the Balloon logo are registered trade marks of Usborne Publishing Limited.
All rights reserved. No part of this publication may be reproduced, stored in a retrieval system, or transmitted in any form or by any means
without prior permission of the publisher. UKE. Printed in China.